Bible Predictions That Make Today's Headlines

By
Phyllis Robinson

Bible Predictions That Make Today's Headlines

Bible Predictions That Make Today's Headlines
by Phyllis Robinson

Printed in the United States of America

ISBN 9781624197260

Unless otherwise indicated, All Scripture quotations are from the New International Version .
Copyright @1973, 1978, 1984, 2011 by Biblica.Inc.

First printing 2012

Dedication

This little booklet is dedicated to the many inmates in our jails and prisons, who, after reading my little book, "Why I Believe the Bible is the Word of God," have asked me to write another. They have tasted that the Lord is good and they want more!

"Taste and see that the Lord is good; blessed is the one who takes refuge in Him."

Psalm 34:8

It is written with thanksgiving for the Prison Chaplains and others like Prison Evangelist, Tony Loeffler, who distributed these books. Only in heaven, when rewards are passed out, will we understand how very special these dedicated people are!

We also want to express our appreciation to Pastor Jack Steves for his suggestions and his very appropriate title—it says it all.

4

Acknowledgements

A wise king once said, *"Plans* fail for lack of counsel, but with many advisers they succeed." (King Solomon in Proverbs 15:22)

My *plan* was to encourage as many people as possible to trust the reliability of God's Word—Our Holy Bible. But, there was no way this could have been accomplished without the counsel and advice of two God-centered men.

Dr. David Reagan is a very busy man with an already full schedule with his popular television program, "Christ in Prophecy," correspondence, trips to Israel, writing his own books, speaking engagements, heading up his yearly Prophecy Conference—the list could fill the pages of this book. Yet, he somehow found the time to offer wise counsel to me concerning, "Bible Predictions that Make Today's Headlines." I am filled with thanksgiving for his counsel and consider him a gift from God. You might want to check out his web site—lamblion.com.

The second God centered man? My husband of 52 years, Ron. His early ministries involved developing computer, proofreading, typesetting and editing skills. Little did he know then that our God would use these skills in his "retirement" years. Patience with me is his most endearing virtue.

I am thankful!

Table of Contents

Bible Predictions That Make Today's Headlines

The Son Times

Romans 13:11 ...now [it is] high **time** to awake out of sleep.

After 20 Centuries...the Jews Come Home

Reporting on General Edmund Allenby's conquest of Jerusalem on December 9, 1917, the *New York Herald* announced in a headline: "Jerusalem is Rescued by British after 673 Years of Moslem Rule." Subtitles then elaborated: "Great Rejoicing in the Christian World" and "Jews Everywhere See the Restoration of Palestine as Part of Allies' Programme."

A London paper, December, 1917 stated, "After 300 years of being held captive by the Turks, Jerusalem was freed by British forces led by Sir Edmund Allenby. While the Turks were busy sealing up the gates of the city, the British made a surprise attack using something new to the Holy City—airplanes!" The 14th Squadron flew low and dropped leaflets instead of bombs. The leaflets read: "Surrender the City" and were signed, General Allenby. Allenby in its Arabic version, becomes Allah-en-Nebi, or "prophet of God." He is known by this Arabic name throughout Palestine. Fearful of this "prophet of God" flying over their heads, the Turks fled and thus freed the City Jerusalem.

10

In the Bible:

As birds flying, so will the LORD of hosts de-fend Jerusalem; defending also he will deliver it; and passing over he will preserve it.

Isaiah 31:5(KJV)

The prophet Isaiah certainly had never seen an air-plane! No wonder he said, "As birds flying..." Yet, our God, who knows the end from the beginning, knew perfectly what Isaiah was seeing!

You can trust Him with your future also.

𝕿𝖍𝖊 𝕾𝖔𝖓 𝕿𝖎𝖒𝖊𝖘

Romans 13:11 ...now [it is] high **time** to awake out of sleep.

State of Israel Is Born

May 16, 1948
Israel Ministry of Foreign Affairs
"The first independent Jewish State in nineteen centuries was born in Tel Aviv as the British Mandate over Palestine came to an end. It was immediately subjected to the test of fire.

"In less than 24 hours the armies of Egypt, Jordan, Syria, Lebanon, and Iraq invaded the country. The newly formed, poorly equipped Israel Defense Forces repulsed the invaders in fierce intermittent fighting which lasted some 15 months and claimed over 6000 Israeli lives.

"Accordingly, the Costal Plain, Galilee and the Negev were in Israel's sovereignty, The West Bank came under Egypt, and the city of Jerusalem was divided, with Jordan controlling the eastern part, and Israel the western sector."

They were off to a rocky start!

In the Bible:

And it shall come to pass in that day, that the Lord shall set his hand again the second time to recover the remnant of his people... and he shall set up an ensign for the nations, and shall assemble the outcasts of Israel and gather together the dispersed of Judah from the four corners of the earth... and the adversaries of Judah shall be cut off.

Isaiah 11:11-13

Yes, this was the second time God recovered "the remnant of His people." The first time, they were recovered from their exile in Babylon. This time they voluntarily left the lands of their exile in the "uttermost parts of the earth."

Never before in the history of mankind has a nation been so dispersed for such a long time—almost 2,000 years. Yet the Israelites returned to their land bringing back ancient customs and beliefs and language.

𝕿he 𝕾on 𝕿imes

Romans 13:11 ...now [it is] high **time** to awake out of sleep.

Flag of the State of Israel Proclaimed

The Provisional Council of State
25 Tishre 5709 (October 1948)

"The Provisional Council of State hereby proclaims that the flag of the State of Israel shall be illustrated as described below:...The background is white and on it are two stripes of sky-blue,...In the middle of the white background between the two blue stripes...is a Star of David..."

The star of David became prominent in the 19th century. According to Gershom Sholem, the motive for the use of the Star of David was the need for a symbol of Judaism parallel to the cross—something to adorn the walls of the modern Jewish house of worship.

In the Bible:

*In that day the Root of Jesse will stand as a
banner (flag) for the peoples.*

Isaiah 11:10

*He lifts up a banner (flag) for the distant na-
tions, He whistles for those at the ends of the
earth.*

Isaiah 5:26

"In that day." What day? As you study Isaiah Chapter
11 you realize that he was writing about the day when
God would gather the children of Israel from the distant nations where they had been scattered.

And who was Jesse? Jesse was King David's father. In
the Book of Isaiah, written approximately 2600 years
ago, we are told that the banner or flag that will beckon
the children of Israel back to their homeland will be
identified with King David!

Isn't it interesting that the "Star of David" never
showed up until the 19th century—just in time for "that
day."

In a changing world you can trust God's unchanging
Word!

Romans 13:11 ...now [it is] high **time** to awake out of sleep.

Jewish Genetics

Wikipedia 2010
"Biologist Robert Pollack stated in 2003 that one cannot determine the biological 'Jewishness' of an individual because there are no DNA sequences common to all Jews and absent from all non-Jews. (But within six years that changed.)

"A 2009 study was able to genetically identify individuals with full or partial Ashkenazi Jewish ancestry. Since... the beginning of the century, geneticists have worked on the Y chromosome (transmitted from father to son) and mitochondrial DNA (transmitted from mother to child), which have the characteristic to be transmitted in full.

"It is therefore *now* (my word added for emphasis) possible to trace the common ancestors of various peoples of the world and especially those of Jewish populations."

In The Bible:

...go your way, Daniel, because the words are closed up and sealed until the time of the end.
                                        Daniel 12:9:

Just a few short years ago it was impossible to accurately determine if a person was truly Jewish. Now, modern testing can even determine if they are from the tribe of Levi!

Have you read the book of Daniel? There was a time when people thought this book was written long after the time of Daniel because the prophecies in it were so historically accurate. But, God told Daniel that "not until the time of the end" would we be able to understand the things Daniel saw. So it is with all of the Old Testament prophets. Just think about all of the prophecies we are seeing in this little book that could not be understood until the development of modern technology.

Could this be the time of the end? You decide.

𝔗𝔥𝔢 𝔖𝔬𝔫 𝔗𝔦𝔪𝔢𝔰

Romans 13:11 ...now [it is] high **time** to awake out of sleep.

Bill to Make Hebrew Sole Official Language

Gabe Kahn
Wikimedia Commons

"The Hebrew language, which became extinct for centuries, as it was not spoken after the Biblical times, was revived in the late 19th century. (Jewish people returned to Israel speaking their various native languages.) The (Hebrew) language now is the most widely spoken language in Israel...several rules and language policies have given the language the honor of the prime status among the languages of Israel.

"Now Hebrew has been adopted as the language of all official correspondence, from the debates in the Israeli Parliaments to the judicial courts."

In the Bible:

For then will I turn to the people a pure language, that they may all call upon the name of the LORD, to serve Him with one consent.
Zephaniah 3:9 (KJV)

In 1881, Eliezer Ben-Yehuda moved with his wife to Jerusalem. Eliezer worked 18 hours a day for 41 years to restore to life the Hebrew language—that language which had been "dead" for 1,700 years. Now it is the official language of Israel.

Think about it. My Dad's parents came to the United States from the Ukraine as newlyweds. I never heard my father speak Ukrainian. Well, alright, he did use to say, "Give me a kiss" in the language of his parents. But I, just the second generation from my grandparents, would not know how to properly pronounce those words or write them here. Yet, after almost 2,000 years of being scattered from one end of the earth to the other, the Jewish people are speaking the language of their forefathers.

No nation speaks ancient Greek but today Israel speaks the ancient language—Hebrew. Why? Because God said they would!

The Son Times

Romans 13:11 ...now [it is] high **time** to awake out of sleep.

Chinese Jews in Israel

Meet Jin Jin Jing! Jin Jin is a Chinese Jew from Kaifeng, China living in Israel. That's right, a Chinese Jew! But, how can this be?

According to Michael Freund, Chairman of Shavei Israel, "There was a Jewish community in Kaifeng for over a thousand years. Jews first arrived there around the eighth or ninth century along the silk route."

Jin Jin, says, "When I was a little child, my father always told me, 'You are Jewish, you should go back to Israel,' so I said, 'ok, I am Jewish, I should go back to Israel.'" She had always wondered why they were not supposed to eat pork, why their graves were different and why they had a mezuzah on their door.

Jin Jin has learned to speak Hebrew. She can now translate Jewish scriptures into Chinese to help the Jewish community in Kaifeng.

Jin Jin now says, "I think my father is right, there is a land that God promised to us. Yes, it is our home."

In the Bible:

Behold, these shall come from far: and, lo, these from the north and from the west; and these from the land of **Sinim.**

Isaiah 49:12 KJV

This ancient prophecy concerning Israel's return to her land in the latter days comes as quite a surprise. What, Jews coming back to Israel from the remote mountains of China?! It was no surprise to Jin Jin and her family and neighbors.

According to Timothy Tow of Far Eastern Bible College, one who is well versed in Chinese is called a Sinologue and sinology is the study of the Chinese language. The war between China and Japan was called the Sino-Japanese war. The translations of the Chinese Bible translate the land of **sinim** as "Chin" which is the root word for China.

𝔗𝔥𝔢 𝔖𝔬𝔫 𝔗𝔦𝔪𝔢𝔰

Romans 13:11 ...now [it is] high **time** to awake out of sleep.

Return of the Russian Jews

From *Why Israel?*
"Ever since the formation of the State of Israel in 1948, the Jewish community in the former Soviet-Union tried to get permission to leave their country to go to Israel. The Soviet authorities treated the Jews as criminals. It was forbidden for them to confess their faith openly. Many of them were imprisoned. Continuous pressure from the West finally made a change.

"During the 1970's and 80's, 160,000 Russian Jews managed to make *Aliyah*."* After the downfall of communism in 1989, the stream of Russian Jews grew enormously."

According to *Wikipedia*, the 2012 census showed 892,400 Russian Jews living in Israel.

About 40,000 Jewish immigrants from the whole world arrive every year in their new homeland of Israel.

*the Jewish word for immigration to Israel

22

In The Bible:

Do not be afraid, for I am with you; I will bring your children from the east and gather you from the west. <u>I will</u> <u>say to the north, "Give them up!"</u> and to the south, "Do not hold them back." Bring my sons from afar and my daughters from the ends of the earth...

Isaiah 43:5

How interesting—God told the north to "give them up!" Russia was the one place where the Jews were not allowed to freely return to Israel. The first returning Jews to Palestine came primarily from eastern Arab countries. The next major movement came from the western countries of Europe, especially Germany. Then, in the early 1990's, great numbers came from Russia in the North. The last great migrations of Jews returning to Israel came from Ethiopia in the south.

This <u>precise order of return</u> was predicted by Isaiah the prophet.

𝔗he 𝔖on 𝔗imes

Romans 13:11 ...now [it is] high **time** to awake out of sleep.

Notes from Jewish South America

JUFNEWS
By Cindy Sher. Managing Editor
"South America has a rich Jewish history, one that most Jews outside of Latin America know little about...In addition to making some new Jewish friends in Uruguay and Argentina, I got to eat some world-famous Argentine (kosher) steak, take in a Tango show, and brush up on my college Spanish...Salud!

"David Telias was born in Montevideo, Uruguay, but has traveled back and forth between Israel and Uruguay his whole life. At age 10, he made aliyah with his family for one year. 'In those days, I did not understand why we did this, but I never could get it out of my mind,' he said. 'It was the first time I asked myself what it means to be Jewish.'"

In the Bible:

Hear the word of the LORD, O nations;
proclaim it in distant coastlands:
"He who scattered Israel will gather
them and will watch over his flock like
a shepherd."

Jeremiah 31:10

For my commentary on this verse I would like to quote from my little book, *Why I Believe the Bible is the Word of God*. "The great missionary and Bible teacher, Lester Sumrall, told this story: He was traveling deep in the jungles of South America where there were no roads and few people. He came upon a shack with a sign on the front indicating it was a store, so he went in. Inside he found that it was sparsely stocked with a few canned goods. Behind the counter he saw a man with a yarmulke on the back of his head reading the Hebrew Scriptures. The missionary asked the Jewish man, 'What in the world are you doing here?' The gentleman responded, 'Waiting to sell you something!'"

When God said, "distant lands" who would have thought—all the way from Israel to South America!

𝕿𝖍𝖊 𝕾𝖔𝖓 𝕿𝖎𝖒𝖊𝖘

Romans 13:11 ...now [it is] high **time** to awake out of sleep.

Last Ethiopian Jews To Return To Israel

June 8, 2011 JERUSALEM, ISRAEL (*Worthy News*)
"A Christian group said Tuesday, June 7, 2008 it would help organize 'the return of the last 8,700 Ethiopian Jews to Israel' by sponsoring what are known as 'Aliyah' flights, in the coming months.

"The Jerusalem-based International Christian Embassy Jerusalem (ICEJ) told *Worthy News* it was asked for urgent assistance by the Jewish Agency, which claims to have brought over three million Jews to Israel since the state's establishment in 1948.

"ICEJ Director of Aliyah Operations, Howard Flower, called the Ethiopians' Aliyah (the Jewish word for *immigration* to Israel) 'urgent, given the current drought and political turmoil in the region.'"

In The Bible:

Let's take another look at Isaiah 43:5:

> *Do not be afraid, for I am with you; I will bring your children from the east and gather you from the west. I will say to the north, "Give them up!"* <u>*and to the south,*</u> *"Do not hold them back." Bring my sons from afar and my daughters from the ends of the earth...*

Now isn't *this* interesting! Once Israel became a nation, Jewish people quickly began leaving their homes in Iran and surrounding lands (the East). Then followed the German Jews (the West) and other western nations. The holocaust was the driving force to get that group moving. Then came the fall of the Soviet Union when Jews were able to freely leave Russia. Then, following the *exact* order given by the prophet Isaiah, they came from the South!

How did Isaiah know the exact order of this "second Exodus"? He didn't, but God did!

The Son Times

Romans 13:11 ...now [it is] high **time** to awake out of sleep.

The Perfect Storm

The front-page headlines of *USA Today* on November 1, 1991 had the stories of the Madrid conference and the "Perfect Storm" next to each other. As President George H. W. Bush was opening the Madrid Conference with the purpose of getting Israel to give up land for peace, one of the most powerful storms ever, as described by meteorologists, was develop-ing in the North Atlantic. It created the largest waves ever recorded in that region. This storm traveled 1,000 miles from east to west instead of the normal west to east pattern where it hit and destroyed major portions of President Bush's Kennebunkport property and home.

In The Bible:

*On that day when the nations of the earth are
gathered against her, I will make Jerusalem
an immovable rock for all the nations. All who
try to move it <u>will injure themselves</u>.*

Zechariah 12:3

You may be thinking, oh, come on, storms happen! Yes,
storms happen but how many turn around in the middle of the Atlantic Ocean and head in the opposite di-
rection and hit President Bush's house at the very mo-
ment he is trying to persuade Israel to "give up land for
peace"?

I might accept that "storms happen" idea if this was
just an isolated incident. There are actually too many to
list but I will mention one more in our next headline.
Do you remember that verse in Mark 4:41 when Jesus'
disciples asked, "Who is this? Even the winds obey
him." He can bring peace to the raging sea for those
who obey Him and destruction for those who disobey
his Word concerning Israel.

The Son Times

Romans 13:11 ...now [it is] high **time** to awake out of sleep.

Hurricane Katrina

America watched with baited breath as Hurricane Katrina, churning in the Gulf of Mexico, threatened New Orleans and Mississippi. Ultimately 1,836 people perished and hundreds of thousands were forced from their homes.

This would prove to be one of the most devastating hurricanes in terms of lives lost in United States history. Loss of homes and businesses made it one of the costliest storms yet recorded.

The residents of New Orleans were forced by this storm to leave their homes the <u>same day</u> as the last residents of Gaza were forced from *their* homes with the endorsement of the United States government.

In the Bible:

On that day the Lord made a covenant with Abram and said, "To your descendants I give this land, from the Wadi of Egypt to the great river, Euphrates."

Genesis 15:18

Hurricane Katrina—coincidence or judgment?

Rabbi Joseph Garlitzky, head of Tel Aviv synagogue, said: "We don't have prophets who can tell us exactly what are God's ways, but when we see something so enormous as Katrina, I would say Bush and Rice need to make an accounting of their actions, because something was done wrong by America in a big way. And here there are many obvious connections between the storm and the Gaza evacuation, <u>which came right on top of each other.</u> No one has permission to take away one inch of the land of Israel from the Jewish people."

Forcing God's people out of the land He has chosen for them is not a good idea!

The Son Times

Romans 13:11 ...now [it is] high **time** to awake out of sleep.

Hijacked Jets Destroy Twin Towers

September 11. 2001
Hijackers flew jetliners into each of New York's World Trade Center towers. They brought down the two 110 story towers

Tuesday morning, September 11. Hundreds were killed aboard the jets or lost their lives in the rubble of the towers. The exact count is unknown.

People were seen jumping out of windows rather than face death by fire.

President Bush stated, "Today our nation saw evil." He continued, "Thousands of lives were ended by evil, despicable acts of terror."

In the Bible:

The bricks are fallen down, but we will build with hewn stones...

Isaiah 9:10

The verse above is the Israelite's response to a "terrorist" attack they had just experienced from the Assyrians from whom the current terrorists are descended. The Bible teaches that God allowed this attack because the Israelites' had turned their backs on Him. So, did they turn back to God? No, in defiance they said, "We will rebuild." *They did not see the attack as God's judgment.*

Now, fast forward to 9-11-2001. Senator Tom Daschle, in a speech on September 12, 2001 said, "There is a passage in the Bible, from Isaiah, that I think, speaks to all of us at times such as this: 'The bricks have fallen down, but we will rebuild.'"

Rudy Giuliani said, "We will rebuild: We're going to come out of this stronger than before..." Donald Trump added, "What I want to see built is the World Trade Centers stronger and maybe a story taller..." Two other political figures also quoted from Isaiah 9:10. Just like the Israelites, *they did not see the attack as God's judgment.*

𝔗𝔥𝔢 𝔖𝔬𝔫 𝔗𝔦𝔪𝔢𝔰

Romans 13:11 ...now [it is] high **time** to awake out of sleep.

Temple Mount Dispute

Myths & Facts Online:Jerusalem
"During the 2000 Camp David Summit, Yasser Arafat said that no Jewish Temple ever existed on the Temple Mount. A year later, the Mufti of Jerusalem, said, *There is not [even] the smallest indication of the existence of a Jewish temple on this place in the past. In the whole city, there is not even a single stone indicating Jewish history.*

"The Zionist movement has invented that this was the site of Solomon's Temple. But this is all a lie."

"These views are contradicted by a book entitled, *A Brief Guide to al-Haram al-Sharif,* published by the Supreme Moslem Council in 1930. The Council, the principal Muslim authority in Jerusalem during the British Mandate, wrote in the guide that the Temple Mount site 'is one of the oldest in the world. Its sanctity dates from the earliest times. Its identity with the site of Solomon's Temple is beyond dispute. This, too, is the spot, according to universal belief, on which 'David built there an altar unto the Lord, and offered burnt offerings and peace offerings.'"

In The Bible:

The supreme Muslim Counsel was actually quoting from 1 Chronicles 22:1 where, speaking of the Temple Mount which he had just purchased, King David said:

> *The house of the Lord God (The Temple) is to be here, and also the <u>altar of burnt offering</u> for Israel.*

While the current inhabitants are removing all the artifacts under the Temple Mount that would confirm Israel's history there, wise students are learning the truth from a book written by the supreme Muslim Council! Proverbs 16:4 tells us that the Lord works out everything for His own ends—He even uses those who do not know Him.

The Son Times

Romans 13:11 ...now [it is] high **time** to awake out of sleep.

Ahmadinejad: Destroy Israel

By Sean Yoong
The Associated Press

"Iranian President Mahmoud Ahmadinejad has declared the solution to the Middle East crisis is to *destroy Israel. He said,* 'The main solution is for the elimination of the Zionist regime...'"

(Note: Many news sources reported that Ahmadinejad had said that Israel must be wiped off the map. It has been argued that no such idiom exists in Persian.)

"The Ahmadinejad's phrase was, according to the text, published on the President's Office's website. This has been corrected to say, 'The Imam said that this regime occupying Jerusalem must [vanish from] the page of time *(bayad az safheh-ye ruzgar mahv shavad).*'"

The Middle East Media Research Institute (MEMRI) translated the phrase similarly, as "this regime" must be "eliminated from the pages of history."

In the Bible:

O God, do not keep silent; be not quiet, O God, be not still.

See how your enemies are astir, how your foes rear their heads.

With cunning they conspire against your people; they plot against those you cherish.

"Come," they say, "let us <u>destroy</u> them as a nation, that the name of Israel be remembered no more."

With one mind they plot together; they form an alliance against you (Israel) the tents of Edom and the Ishmaelites.

Psalm 83:1-6

In the margin of my Bible I have written right next to verse 4, "Ahmadinejad plagiarized!" Indeed he did. He plagiarized the Word of God.

Notice who Israel's enemies were—the tents of Edom and the Ishmaelites—both ancestors of today's modern Arabs—and of Mahmoud Ahmadinejad!

The Son Times

Romans 13:11 ...now [it is] high **time** to awake out of sleep.

Smart Missiles

Stars and Stripes
by Warren Peace
"The combat zone just got a little more high-tech as soldiers in Afghanistan began testing and training on five prototype weapons that fire smart bullets. Smart weapons have some form of a processing unit that allows them to be self-guided or, in this case, have self-adjusting sights and programmable rounds.

"The XM25 -- which is not much bigger than a standard service rifle -- fires 25 mm rounds that can be programmed to explode on impact, in front of or behind an object. The weapon allows soldiers to kill enemies hiding behind walls or other cover by firing above, or to the side, of the wall from up to 700 meters away."

"A Sidewinder missile weaves through the air toward an enemy target as if it has a mind of its own -- and in a way, it does."
(How Stuff Works)

In the Bible:

*Their arrows will be like skilled warriors
who do not return empty handed.*
Jeremiah 50:9

Thank God for Biblical scholars who look into the original text to find gems like this one. In this verse the original language, Hebrew, denotes "<u>the intelligence is in the arrow.</u>"

Jeremiah 50 is all about the end-times. It looks as if the world is well prepared for that day.

Now, how do you suppose God knew about "smart missiles" way back in the days when bows and arrows were pretty much the only weapons?

The Son Times

Romans 13:11 ...now [it is] high **time** to awake out of sleep.

First Atomic Bomb Dropped on Japan

From newspapers across America
On August 6, 1945, President Truman (in his speech to the people of America) announced that an atomic bomb, possessing more power than 20,000 tons of TNT and more than 2,000 times the blast power of what previously was the world's most devastating bomb, had been dropped on Hiroshima, Japan.

The announcement, first given to the world in utmost solemnity by President Truman, made it plain that the "age of atomic energy," which can be a tremendous force for the advancement of civilization as well as for destruction, was at hand.

In the Bible:

If those days had not been cut short, no one would survive, but for the sake of the elect those days will be shortened.

Matthew 24:22

Imagine what you might have thought when Jesus spoke these words 2,000 years ago. What? Wipe out the world's population with bows and arrows and spears? I don't think so.

Only in our lifetime have weapons been developed that could wipe out the whole world. What you read in secular books today is often speculation. What you read in God's Word, no matter how impossible it may seem, you can be sure is true.

The Son Times

Romans 13:11 ...now [it is] high **time** to awake out of sleep.

Turkey will Cut off Flow Of Euphrates

The Indianapolis Star
January 13, 1990
"'Turkey Will Cut Off Flow of Euphrates for One Month.' A huge reservoir has been built by Turkey. While filling up the reservoir, the flow of the Euphrates will be stopped for one month and a concrete plug for a diversion channel built..."

The Shrinking Euphrates

Drought in the area of the Euphrates has left the giant river smaller than it ever has been. According to the New York Times, "The shrinking of the Euphrates, a river so crucial to the birth of civilization, that *the Book of Revelation prophesied its drying up as a sign of the end times*, (emphasis mine) has decimated farms along its banks." Fisherman are suffering financially and riverside farmers are having to flee to the cities to find employment.

In The Bible:

The sixth angel poured out his bowl on the great river Euphrates, and its water was dried up to prepare the way for the kings from the East.

Revelation 16:12

Who could have imagined in the Apostle John's day, a 1700 mile long river drying up! Perhaps God Himself will continue to withhold water from that mighty river. Or, perhaps the great dams built by Turkey will be responsible for the ability of the "Kings of the East" to cross this river. Then we must ask ourselves, "What or Who inspired the Turks to go to such great expense to make the drying of the Euphrates possible?"

Even the New York Times writer saw the significance of this Bible prophecy. Do you?

𝔗𝔥𝔢 𝔖𝔬𝔫 𝔗𝔦𝔪𝔢𝔰

Romans 13:11 ...now [it is] high **time** to awake out of sleep.

The Birds of Armageddon

The Jerusalem Post (October 1, 1988)
"Each fall, billions of birds around the world...rise from their nests at a given hour and head south like retired New York couples heading for Florida."

According to BBC News, "Every autumn, over 500 million birds cross Israel's airspace, heading south to warming weather in Africa." There are nearly 300 species of birds whose arrival can be predicted "almost to the day."

Vultures, birds that feed on carrion, are suddenly increasing dramatically in Israel.

According to Wikipedia, "Colonies of Griffon Vultures can be found in northern Israel and in the Golan Heights, where a large colony breeds in the Carmel Mountains."

Residents are setting up nesting and feeding stations for vultures throughout Israel which is increasing the vulture population.

In the Bible:

And I saw an angel standing in the sun, who cried in a loud voice to all the birds flying in midair, "Come, gather together for the great supper of God..."

Revelation 19:17

Son of man, this is what the Sovereign LORD says: "Call out to <u>every kind of bird</u> and all the wild animals: Assemble and come together from all around to the sacrifice I am preparing for you, the great sacrifice on the <u>mountains of Israel</u>. There you will eat flesh and drink blood."

Ezekiel 39:17

These verses speak of the "cleanup job" which must be done at the end of the Battle of Armageddon where there will be the greatest slaughter of the enemies of Israel ever known to mankind. Please notice that Wikipedia stated that the vultures were breeding in northern Israel and in the "Golan Heights in the Carmel Mountains."

It seems like our God is getting ready for something!

𝔗𝔥𝔢 𝔖𝔬𝔫 𝔗𝔦𝔪𝔢𝔰

Romans 13:11 ...now [it is] high **time** to awake out of sleep.

Ancient Document Confirms Existence Of Biblical Figure

By NIGEL REYNOLDS,
The Daily Telegraph
LONDON
"The sound of unbridled joy seldom breaks the quiet of the British Museum's great Arched Room, which holds its collection of 130,000 Assyrian cuneiform tablets, dating back 5,000 years.

"But Michael Jursa, a visiting professor from Vienna, let out such a cry last Thursday. He had made what has been called the most important find in biblical archaeology for 100 years, a discovery that supports the view that the historical books of the Bible are based on fact.

"Searching for Babylonian financial accounts among the tablets, Jursa suddenly came across a name that he half remembered — Nabushar-russu-ukin, described there in 2,500-year-old writing as 'the chief eunuch' of Nebuchadnezzar II, king of Babylon. The name translated, Nebo-Sarsekim, was Nebuchadnezzar II's 'chief officer.'"

In The Bible:

*Then all the officials of the king of Babylon
came and took seats in the Middle Gate...Nebo
-Sareskim a chief officer...and all the rest of
the officials of the king of Babylon.*

Jeremiah 39:3

An obscure detail in the Old Testament turns out to be accurate and true. As Irving Finkel, a British Museum expert says, "I think that it means that the whole of the narrative [of Jeremiah] takes on a new kind of power." And, as Bible scholar, Phillip Goodman wrote, "The person and title, the time and place all fit perfectly with the Bible."

This reminds me of another verse in the Bible: "Go your way, Daniel,...until the time of the end. Many will be purified, made spotless and refined, but...None of the wicked will understand." Daniel 12:9

Are you among the purified, spotless and refined? Jesus said He is coming back for a bride who is without spot or wrinkle. (Ephesians 5:27). Best of all, He is the One who cleanses you!

𝔗he 𝔖on 𝔗imes

Romans 13:11 ...now [it is] high **time** to awake out of sleep.

Dead Sea Mystery

Jerusalem Post
September 22, 2011
"A Ben-Gurion University research team discovered *fresh water underground springs that have promoted new types of microorganisms.* Never before have microbial mats/biofilms been found in the Dead Sea...."

From *Our Amazing Planet*:
"For the first time, researchers have sent a diving expedition into the Dead Sea where they uncovered fresh water.

"In addition, the divers found mats of microbes living near the holes in the seafloor. The variety of the microorganisms living in an environment thought to be largely devoid of life was surprising, the researchers said.

"...carpets of microorganisms that cover large seafloor areas contain considerable richness of species, said Danny Ionescu of the Max Planck Institute for Marine Microbiology in Germany, an institute that collaborated with the Israeli researchers on the recent expedition."

In the Bible:

...this water goes down into the Arabah, (Jordan Valley) where it enters the sea. (Dead Sea). Swarms of <u>living creatures</u> will live wherever the river flows. There will be large fish, because this water flows there and <u>makes the salt water fresh</u>; so where the river flows everything will live."...<u>But the swamps and marshes will not become fresh; they will be left for salt.</u> *

Ezekiel 47:8-11*

*My *New Defender's Study Bible* notes suggests that this river is coming from "subterranean reservoirs."

Wait! Did we just read in Ezekiel's vision that during the millennium the water of the Dead Sea will become fresh and people will fish there? And did we also read in Ezekiel's vision that one end of the sea would stay salty? Sure enough, that's what it says!

While this verse speaks of the millennium it encourages me to know that it is no problem for our God to bring this about. The several recent scientific reports published lately on this subject further encourages me that the time for the fulfillment of Ezekiel's vision is rapidly approaching.

The Son Times

Romans 13:11 ...now [it is] high **time** to awake out of sleep.

Rahab's House?

As long as there have been archeologists there have been people digging at the ruins of the City of Jericho. The digging was halted in 1994 when the area was under the control of the Palestinians.

In the Spring of 1997, two Italian archaeologists who were commissioned to work there suddenly left after one month declaring that they found no evidence for a destruction from the time of Joshua. *christiananswers.net*

The next Fall, Dr. Bryant Wood, Director of the Associates for Biblical Research, visited Jericho and found the Italians had uncovered a **still intact section of the wall not yet discovered in the history of former digs!** As the biblical story goes, God caused the walls of Jericho to fall—all except the part where Rahab's house stood.

The Italian's sudden exodus brings up the possibility that the Palestinian Authority supported their dig for the purpose of denouncing any Jewish connection to the site.

In The Bible:

> *By faith the walls of Jericho fell, after the people had marched around them for seven days. By faith the prostitute Rahab, because she welcomed the spies, was not killed with those who were disobedient.*
>
> Hebrews 11:30-31
>
> *...the house she lived in was part of the city wall.*
>
> Joshua 2:15

Going back to the early 1900's: "The German excavation of 1907-1909 found that on the north a short stretch of the lower city wall did not fall... A portion of that wall was still standing...(Sellin & Watzinger 1973: 58). What is more, there were houses built against the wall! It is quite possible that this is where Rahab's house was located. Since the city wall formed the back wall of the houses, the spies could have readily escaped. From this location on the north side of the city, it was only a short distance to the hills of the Judean wilderness where the spies hid for three days (Jos 2:16, 22)." *Associates for Biblical Research*

Isn't it sad that the Italian archeologists were digging at this Biblical site obviously with the purpose of disproving the Bible. They actually lied about their findings!

Archeologists today are constantly uncovering evidence to support the authenticity of our Holy Bible.

The Son Times

Romans 13:11 ...now [it is] high **time** to awake out of sleep.

The Time is Finished

National Post Staff:
May 2, 2012
ST. CATHARINES, ONT.
"Doris Rosado watches her teenage daughters... get the numbers '666' tattooed on their wrists... This St. Catharine's family belongs to an obscure 'Christian' sect for which '666' is a positive symbol of their group's messianic leader. (Quote marks on 'Christian' are mine).

"For this family, and other members of Growing in Grace International, these tattoos are a way of demonstrating their faith as true believers of Jose de Luis de Jesus — who they fervently believe is the second coming of Jesus Christ...

"The group has members in more than 130 countries and believes that on June 30 (or July 1 across the international dateline) their Texas-based leader and his followers will be transformed.

"That day, the body of Jose de Luis de Jesus, who is a human like you and me, his flesh is going to be immortal.... He's going to be living forever. And that will happen to him, but also his followers."

In The Bible:

<u>Many</u> will come in my name, claiming, "I am he," and will deceive many.

Mark 13:6

This comes as no surprise. Do you remember when the declaration came "...to all Heaven and Earth that Reverend Sun Yung Moon is none other than humanity's Savior, Messiah, Returning Lord and True Parent?" Research shows that there are and have been <u>many</u> others. We shake our heads and exclaim, "How can these people be so deceived!" Jesus saw this coming and warned us.

By the way, June 30 and July 1 have come and gone. Yet, the tattoos on Doris Rosado's daughters' wrists remain!

The Son Times

Romans 13:11 ...now [it is] high **time** to awake out of sleep.

Unbelief Unveiled

From: *The Layman* by Rev. Parker T. Williamson

"'I preach on the Bible about as much as any other preacher. I don't preach on it as if it were a book to believe. I don't find most of it particularly believable, at least in the way that we were supposed to believe it...' Preached on March 4, 2012, these are the words of John Shuck, a Presbyterian Church (USA) minister...Shuck is not alone. At the General Assembly, he will find allies who are equally dismissive of God's Word. The Rev. Janet Edwards, a self identified 'bisexual' whose officiating at lesbian wedding ceremonies and has made the news in recent years, will also be there as a voting commissioner...."

In the Bible:

Let no man deceive you by any means for that day (the return of Jesus) shall not come except there come a falling away first...

2 Thessalonians 2:3

However, when the Son of Man comes will He find faith on the earth?

Luke 18:8

John Knox, founder of the Presbyterian Church and considered to be the greatest Reformer in the history of Scotland, would "roll over in his grave" as the saying goes, if he could see what is happening today in the Presbyterian Church USA. Here are the words spoken at his funeral: "Here lyeth a man who in his life never feared the face of man, who hath been often threatened with dagger, but yet hath ended his dayes in peace and honour." The church he founded does not seem to be ending it's days in peace and honor as Biblically faithful Presbyterians by the ten of thousands are heading for the exit."

𝔗𝔥𝔢 𝔖𝔬𝔫 𝔗𝔦𝔪𝔢𝔰

Romans 13:11 ...now [it is] high **time** to awake out of sleep.

Arab Spring More Like Winter of Discontent

The scene is becoming quite familiar in the Middle East—Arab fighting Arab as one regime after another topples.

Angry mobs in the streets of Cairo ended the 32-year reign of Hosni Mubarak.

Similar scenes have taken place in Libya where Colonel Khaddafi was killed by angry mobs of his own people.

It looks as if President Bashar Assad of Syria may be next. New Muslim leadership is rising up in many of these Arab states.

This civil resistance began in Tunisia and led to the ousting of longtime President Zine El Abidine Ben Ali. Thus began the Arab Spring.

Since then we have seen similar actions in Bahrain and Yemen as well as elsewhere in North Africa and the Middle East.

In the Bible:

Nation will rise against nation, and kingdom against kingdom.

Matthew 24:7

I will stir up Egyptian against Egyptian— brother will fight against brother, neighbor against neighbor, city against city, kingdom against kingdom.

Isaiah 19:2

Jesus' disciples asked him what would be the sign of His coming and of the end of the age. (Matthew 24:2). Part of Jesus' answer was, "Nation will rise against nation." The original Greek word translated "nation" was "*ethnos,*" from which we get our word "*ethnic*". In other words, ethnic group will rise against ethnic group. To make it even more plain—Libyan against Libyan, Syrian against Syrian, Egyptian against Egyptian—as in today's headlines!!

𝔗𝔥𝔢 𝔖𝔬𝔫 𝔗𝔦𝔪𝔢𝔰

Romans 13:11 ...now [it is] high **time** to awake out of sleep.

Where Has All The Money Gone?

The long predicted "Paperless Society" never did come. Our desks, tables, and sometimes floors are littered! But then there was the prediction of the "Cashless Society." According to the *Center for research of Globalization,* "Over the years, futurists and commentators alike seemed to agree that a cashless society will be a slow creep, and would automatically phase itself in simply by virtue of the sheer volume of electronic transactions that would

gradually make cash less available and more costly to redeem or exchange." Now that's an entirely different picture.

The uninformed walk into a hotel, cash in hand, thinking to rent a room. That just will not happen. Rent a car to get there without a credit card? The first thing you will be asked for in either situation is your credit card number.

58

In the Bible:

He also forced everyone, small and great, rich
and poor, free and slave, to receive a mark on
his right hand or on his forehead, so that no
one could buy or sell unless he had the mark...

Revelation 13: 16,17

Nearly every human being in the world now has been assigned a number. In America it is our Social Security number. Even a child without a Social Security number cannot be declared as a dependent on an income tax return. Not until the advent of the computer could this have been accomplished.

"Buy or sell"—have you tried to rent a car or get a hotel room with cash lately? You can't even get through the turnstiles at Disney World without using their fingertip biometrics!

The Son Times

Romans 13:11 ...now [it is] high **time** to awake out of sleep.

Upgraded Missile Technology

Israel is upgrading its 'Arrow II' missile shield over fears of possible attacks by Iran and Syria. The 'Block-4' up-grade is currently being installed and deployed across the country, according to a senior Israeli defense official.

The upgrade has greater accuracy and the ability to intercept missiles even further away.

It is part of the technological race in the Middle East.

Jerusalem is now developing the Arrow III. The Arrow III system will engage incoming missiles in space, using detachable payloads that zero in on their target.

Israel is working on even more powerful interceptor technology, known as David's Sling or Magic Wand.

In the Bible:

But you, Daniel, roll up and seal the words of the scroll (Old Testament book) until the time of the end. Many will go here and there to increase knowledge."

Daniel 12:4, 9ff.

There is no doubt that knowledge is increasing these days with new technology in travel, science (including computer science), and medical science.

But here's the good part. Michael, the angel who was talking to Daniel, said, "'Go your way Daniel...until the time of the end.' Many will be purified, made spotless and refined but the wicked will continue to be wicked. None of the wicked will understand, but those who are *wise* will understand." (Daniel 12:9-10)

Have you been *wise* and made sure of your eternal destiny? While secular knowledge is increasing so also is our ability so put the "time of the end" into perspective. Just keep one eye on the Headlines and the other on your Bible!

𝔗𝔥𝔢 𝔖𝔬𝔫 𝔗𝔦𝔪𝔢𝔰

Romans 13:11 ...now [it is] high **time** to awake out of sleep.

State of Texas Hit Hard by West Nile Virus

The city of Arlington, Texas is encouraging its residents to protect themselves from potentially deadly mosquito bites as the number of reported West Nile virus cases there climbed to 39.

Labor Day weekend outdoor activities were hampered by "lock-ins" as airplanes blanketed Dallas residents with toxic chemicals to kill mosquitoes carrying the deadly West Nile Virus. However, spraying is not entirely effective since mosquitoes breed so quickly the spraying must be repeated every couple of days.

Texas residents have been advised to dress in long sleeves and pants, use insect repellent and drain standing water on their property to avoid infection.

In the Bible:

There will be great earthquakes, famines and pestilences in various places, and fearful events and great signs from heaven.

Luke 21:11

Yes, the Bible speaks about last days pestilences. And, perhaps the West Nile Virus, or the Bird Flu, Aids, and Swine Flu are reminders of what is to come.

My sister Bev, loves to quote a preacher friend who says, "Brethren, it is getting gloriously dark!" The wars, the violence, the plagues must come to a fallen world where Satan "is filled with fury because he knows that his time is short." (Revelation 12:21) But for those who have been cleansed by the sacrificial blood of Christ there is HOPE!

The Son Times

Romans 13:11 ...now [it is] high **time** to awake out of sleep.

Colorado School Seizes Rosary Beads From Student, Calls Them "Gang" Symbol

Published September 15, 2012
FoxNews.com
"Officials at a Colorado high school reportedly confiscated rosary beads from a student, claiming the religious necklace is affiliated with gangs and disruptive to learning.

"Manuel Vigil, a 16-year-old junior at Thompson Valley High School in Loveland, said administrators offered no explanation when they seized the rosary beads twice since school started three weeks ago, Fox affiliate KDVR reported.

"'They tell me I can't wear them,' Vigil told the station, adding that he wears the beads to protect himself from harm.

"'I use them for prayer. I feel safe when I have them on,' he said."

In the Bible:

Woe to those who call evil good and good evil, who put darkness for light and light for darkness, who put bitter for sweet and sweet for bitter.

Isaiah 5:20

The word "woe" in the Bible means great distress, regret or grief. Think of the many people today who call those who believe in salvation through Jesus Christ, "narrow minded." Or, worse, your Catholic friend's rosary a gang symbol. God warns these people that they will one day regret the stand they took against what is good.

All who reject the Bible as God's message to us will surely face great distress, regret and grief when they stand before our Holy God.

Conclusion

WHY DID GOD PREDICT?

Our Holy Bible is full of predictions like the ones you have just read. "These are written that you may believe that Jesus is the Messiah, the Son of God, and that by believing you may have life in His name. (John 20:31)

This, then, would indicate that these Bible predictions found in today's headlines were not just for our entertainment or to fill our heads with more facts. But, rather to make sure that we know that Jesus is the Son of God, and that by believing in Him we may have everlasting life.

In 1 John 5:13 we read, "I write these things to you who believe in the name of the Son of God so that you may <u>know</u> that you have eternal life." Perhaps you already believe in the name of Jesus but you need assurance that you have eternal life. Search the Scriptures! Get to know Him and His Word. Keep watching for more Bible prophecies in today's Headlines—one eye on breaking news the other eye your Bible!

But what if you have never believed that Jesus is the Son of God and that He can give you eternal life? These predictions (or prophecies) have been written so that "by believing you may have life in His name."

I would like to suggest that you pray the following prayer, sincerely and from your heart. He will hear you and give you the gift of eternal life:

Father God, I thank you for sending Your Son Jesus Christ to pay the penalty for my sins. I thank You that He rose from the grave to give me eternal life. Forgive me for going my own way. I surrender my life and my future to you. Live Your life in me as You please. Change my heart and my desires. Give me a hunger to know You and Your Word and to live a life that pleases You.

Thank You, Father, for hearing and answering this prayer. In the name of Jesus I pray.

I would like to leave you with my favorite prediction. It was made by Jesus in John 14:3 "...If I go and prepare a place for you, I will come back and take you to be with me that you also may be where I am."

 The Apostle Paul put it this way in I Thessalonians 4:16 and 17, "For the Lord himself will come down from heaven, with a loud command, with the voice of the archangel and with the trumpet call of God, and the dead in Christ will rise first. After that, we who are still alive and are left will be caught up together with them in the clouds to meet the Lord in the air. And so we will be with the Lord forever."

The Bible contains the mind of God, the state of man, the way of salvation, the doom of sinners, and the happiness of believers. Its doctrines are holy, its precepts are binding, its histories are true, and its decisions are immutable. Read it to be wise, believe it to be safe, and practice it to be holy.

From the Gideon Bible Preface

How to Contact the Author
Additional copies of *Bible Predictions That Make Today's Headline*s are available from:

Phyllis Robinson
P.O. Box 1022
Georgetown, TX 78627

**Be sure to check her web site
www.whyibelievebook.com**

You will want to read *Why I Believe the Bible is the Word of God* with over 300,000 copies in distribution.

Author is available for speaking engagements.